Bronwyn Climbed

The Tree

By Heather Edwards

Cover Art by Grant Edwards

ISBN 1456325159

Dedication

For my darling daughter Bronwyn,

Love, Mom

Contents

I

Bronwyn Climbs the Tree

There was a climbing tree in Bronwyn's backyard. Have you ever wondered what makes a tree a 'climbing tree'? It doesn't come out of a package from the store with a label on that says "This tree is for climbing. Children will love it. Ages 10 and up." If you look in the dictionary under "climbing tree" you won't find anything. If you look it up on the Internet, there's not much help there either. But everyone knows that some trees are for climbing, and this was one of them. The branches were like arms that stuck out at just the right angle for sitting on, and its twiggy fingers held the spreading leaves over each seat like an umbrella. Every year its gnarled branches were covered with a cloud of green leaves that rustled and danced in the spring breezes and then shaded the grass below when the summer sun glared down without blinking. The tree waited there like an invitation - so still and silent and patient. It said to Bronwyn every day, "Climb me". And nearly every day, she tried to do just that.

From experience Bronwyn knew that getting up the fat trunk to the first set of branches was the hardest part. Her brothers had done it when they were eight. Her big sister would sit straddled on the lowest arm and say to her in a dreamy voice, "Being up here is so awesome." She told Bronwyn, "Someday you'll be big enough." It was maddening.

Several times she had pulled a lawn chair over to it and tried to hoist herself up that way, but all she ever got out of that was a bump on the head when the chair tipped over backward and threw her to the ground.

When she was eight years old she was left behind while the older children went to summer camp (too young, again!). She was left to wander listlessly through the house and then the yard and then the house again sighing and bored and annoyed.

"Draw a picture," suggested her mother.

"I'm bored with pictures, I already drew three today."

"Read a book," was the next idea. She could have guessed that would come next, it usually did.

"I already read."

Her mother made an exasperated sound and used the last trick on her list of usual replies, "Use your imagination, Bronwyn, and just find something to do outside!"

Outside was hot and no matter where she looked, she couldn't see anything with her imagination. Under the tree was cooler, though, so she wandered into the shade and stood and stared up at the perfect sitting places and glimmering leafy umbrellas just beyond her reach. She knew it was time to try once again to climb it.

"Stupid tree," she muttered as she hugged the barky trunk and managed to scoot up a couple of feet, "Too fat, too tall...OUCH!" She slid back down to the grass and bit her lip when she noticed the trickle of blood running down her knee. On other days she would usually kick the tree and maybe slap it once or twice and then go find something else to do. But today it was the tree or nothing. She saw the plastic lawn chair as it sat there laughing at her, and she made a face at it. She wouldn't fall for that one again. But maybe one of the metal lawn chairs wouldn't be so unpredictable? It was certainly worth a try.

The metal lawn chair was harder to drag but proved to be a much better ladder. She reopened the scab on her knee and made a fresh one on the other side, but this time she got up to the first branch and scooted herself around and sat huffing and sweating in the crook. It was a moment to be proud and she almost wished someone could have been there to see her. Almost, that is, because when she thought about it she realized that her scramble to the first branch hadn't exactly been what Mom would call "decent". Next time she probably wouldn't wear a dress.

The first thing she noticed as she looked down and around the yard was that her sister had been right (you can be annoying and right at the same time, did you know that?). The world looked different. It felt like she was on a ship. She sat and looked all around and then decided to try and move up higher along the branch. Like I said before, the climb up the first part was the hardest and now just to scoot out on the limb was much easier.

When she stopped and sat still again she saw the garage roof from up above for the first time, and it looked strange. In the gutter she could see all the hard work that the sparrows had done that spring. It was a much bigger nest than she had been able to see from the ground. It had twigs and grass and yarn woven into it as well as something bright orange that she was sure was one of her missing hair ties. She'd bring that up next time Mom yelled at her for losing them.

It also had a garden that hung down from it where one of the twigs had sprouted a plant that now grew, dangling down from the nest. She was glad they'd all ganged up on Dad and begged him not to clean the nest out of that gutter. She could see the tiny broken shells that lay in a heap and wondered where the babies were now? Were they already all grown up and flown away? It had been a couple of months since she'd seen the mother bird fly up there with food for her babies. If only people grew up that fast. She would have been up in this tree years ago!

She looked up through the branches to the top of the tree. She remembered when her older brother had climbed all the way to the top. Her mother had looked out the window and then had charged outside in a big rush. She yelled and flapped her arms around like a wet chicken. "You're too high! Be more careful! Look at the size of those limbs, they aren't strong enough! Don't go so near the top! Pay attention to what you're doing! Do you have any idea what it would be like to spend the rest of your life in a wheelchair? You'll have to have someone help you go to the bathroom!"

If any of these things would make him come down, it would have been the last one, but he didn't seem to hear her. He was too far away. He sailed his ship out to sea and saw such surprising things from the top of the mast.

Bronwyn had laughed when he saw her mother cover her eyes with her hands and say, "Well, if he wants to kill himself, who am I to try and stop him?" as she went back inside. Later at dinner, there had been a more detailed discussion about life in a wheelchair. Mom said she just wanted him to make his decisions with all the facts.

She definitely didn't think she'd go all the way to the top, but the next set of branches would be easy enough to get to. Before she tried that, however, she wanted to try to hang upside down from the bottom branch. She had watched her brothers and sister do it many times and heard all the talk about the blood that would drain down into your face and eventually burst out your eyeballs. She wouldn't miss out on that for anything!

It was much scarier than it looked from the ground. Even though she went super slow and held on the branch with her hands until she really had to let go, it was a sudden shock when she fell free and hung there with her knees latched on to the tree's arm. The rough bark scratched the back of her knees. Her arms didn't want to go all the way straight and very quickly her face began to feel full and strange. Her nose tingled and the skin under her hair was bubbly, and in a sudden panic she worried that the blood really would gush out somewhere. Most importantly, that silly dress now hung right over her face.

It was harder to get back up than she thought it would be, and by the time she managed it she was red and sweating again. The back of her knees hurt and judging by the growling in her stomach, it was time for some kind of snack.

You might think that Bronwyn had already had a pretty exciting day after she'd managed to climb into that tree. But as you'll soon see, when she jumped down to go get some lunch, her adventure that day was far from over. In fact, it hadn't even really begun.

II

Pert

"There's leftover lasagna, there's some boiled eggs, there's always peanut butter and jelly..." Mom's head was in the refrigerator.

"I'll have lasagna."

"I see you managed to get up in the tree, you'll be careful up there, right?"

"Yep." She waited to hear about wheelchairs and wearing shorts under her dress, but after she had plopped the plate into the microwave, Mom just got out a band-aid, ripped the paper off, and pressed it onto her bloody knee without a word.

As she ate, Bronwyn thought about how quiet and peaceful it was up in the tree and decided to take some books up there to read. She had a couple she was working on and a couple that she always took along on any reading trip just in case she needed to remember what her favorite books were like. So, when she went out into the bright afternoon again, she had four books tucked under her arm: *Trumpet of the Swan*, her favorite book of all time, *Travels of Thelonius*, because it had cool pictures, *James and the Giant Peach*, which she was in the middle of, and an Agatha Christie mystery - she was "too young for it" according to her sister – so she had to carry it around just in case she became old enough without any warning. You couldn't be too careful. She also would have had the *Complete Adventures of Winnie-the-Pooh* along, but since it was the "complete" adventures, it was too big and heavy.

Getting up again was hard enough, but now with four books under one arm it was quite impossible. She found a bucket in the garage and tied a rope to the handle. When she got up again she pulled the bucket up with the rope and then looked around for the right reading spot. This was the time for moving to the next set of branches. Getting there with the bucket was tricky. When she sat down in the crook she pulled up the bucket, took out *James and the Giant Peach* and then tied the bucket to the branch.

Very quickly she realized that balancing in the tree with the book was a little less comfortable than lying in the grass with a book. After all that work, though, she wasn't about to give up just yet. Thumbing through the pages took both hands, so she had to keep her balance without holding on and this made her heart beat fast. Where were the cloud men? What was happening to James and his friends?

Just when she'd found her place, a noise over her head made her jump a little. Can you imagine how dangerous it is to have a startled jump while sitting in a tree with both your hands on a book? She looked up quickly and saw a squirrel sitting in the next branch with his paws crossed over one another and his head slightly to one side and his tiny black eyes fixed on her. It seemed that he also was startled to see her sitting in the tree. She couldn't be sure, but he didn't seem all that happy about it either.

What happened next will tell you something about the strange "differentness" of being up in a tree. It is a quiet, slightly magical place that makes you think that *anything* could happen. So it seemed quite normal that she should try to be polite and put the little gray creature at ease somehow. It was probably "his" tree.

"Hello there Squirrel. What's your name?" She said it softly and without any hope of an answer, so, when she saw his mouth open and heard a small voice, she really did start to tip over backwards and nearly fell off the branch.

"Pert." It was just one simple word. Perhaps it wasn't a word at all, but just a noise that squirrels make that seemed like a word.

"I'm sorry, did you say your name was Pert?" She knew it couldn't possibly be true, but after reading about all the adventures of James and his friends in the peach, she was secretly hoping that it was.

"Pert, yes, do you need something? I'm very busy!" Its tail was up and ready, and it was obviously in a great rush to be off.

Bronwyn sat and stared with her mouth wide open. She couldn't think of a single word to say. She saw it shift slightly and then, without another word, it bounded up to the next branch. She gasped and thought wildly of what she might say to keep it there and make it talk some more. She blurted out, "You're that bad squirrel!"

This proved to be very effective because before she could count to three it had scurried down the trunk upside down and sat within a few inches of her face with a most indignant expression. "What do you mean by that?"

"I mean, you're the one who keeps stealing our strawberries!"

"I most certainly am not!"

"Yes, you are, I saw you! What's even worse, you always eat only half of a perfectly good strawberry and then throw the rest on the ground!"

"I don't know what you're talking about! Who are you to climb up into my tree and accuse me of being a thief? A *wasteful* thief on top of everything else!" It waved its paws and brushed his tail from side to side in anger.

"Well..." Truthfully Bronwyn didn't really want to make it too angry. She really wanted to be friends, but on the other hand, it did seem unfair that Mom had planted those strawberries and cared for them all spring just to have some cheeky squirrel sneak in when it thought no one was looking and half-way eat the best and reddest ones. This was a delicate situation, and it seemed unfortunate that she should be facing such a tricky conversation when she'd only just started having arguments with real animals (she'd had plenty of arguments with stuffed animals, but she always won those).

"Well, I guess you couldn't help it. You probably didn't even know that those strawberries belonged to us." It was the best thinking she could do on the spur of the moment while balancing on the branch of a tree. Surely the squirrel would see that she was at a disadvantage and give her the point.

"You miserable, wretched little girl!" it squeaked in a rage, "Do you think every squirrel you see is the same one? Do we all look the same to you? Do you go all over the city and see gray squirrels climbing up trees and think that they are all the very same squirrel? How dare you confuse me with that good-for-nothing who lives in the front yard with your precious strawberries?"

"Well, I'm very sorry then. I…" But she got no further before the offended animal darted back up the tree and out of sight. In the hot, silent afternoon breeze she sat and thought hard about meeting a talking squirrel and what it might mean.

Mom might be interested to hear about this, but then what might she say? She might feel her head and ask if she was feeling too hot. She might suggest a nap or something even worse. She decided against mentioning it to her…just in case.

III

The Melancholy Ant

That night, just as she was crawling into bed, it started to rain. The steady drumming on the roof was soon drowned out by rolling claps of thunder. Flashes of lightening flickered through the curtains. Bronwyn grabbed Toto and covered her head with the soft red creature and stuffed the arms and legs into her ears. Her friend was used to this and lay perfectly still – blocking out the sounds of the storm.

Toto was a red fox. Of all the creatures in the animal kingdom, or even the stuffed animal zoo on her bed, foxes were Bronwyn's favorite. She loved her arctic fox and fennec fox very much, but the red fox named Toto was the most honored and loved of all her family of friends. She had even gone with Bronwyn to the hospital just a few weeks earlier when she'd had an asthma attack.

When the thunder died down, Toto ventured to make friendly conversation. Of course Bronwyn could never hide anything from her, so very soon she was telling her all about the strange adventure in the tree.

"A real *breathing* animal?" the fox asked.

"Real and breathing and also quite rude," Bronwyn told her.

"Well, you did accuse him of stealing. You might be rude if someone you'd never met before did that to you."

"Hmmm… I suppose that's true. Maybe tomorrow I'll go up there and apologize."

"You may not even find him there. Squirrels move around a lot. They travel through many different trees and then hide their nuts and seeds in all kinds of different secret hiding places."

"How do you know so much about squirrels? We don't have one here." She glanced around the bed. To be honest, she had so many stuffed animals that there actually could have been a squirrel in there somewhere that she'd forgotten about.

"I heard it in a book. It was *Prince Caspian,* I think."

"I didn't know you could read! Is that what you do when I'm not here?"

"I didn't read it, I listened to your mother read it to us, remember?"

It was true. She always had Toto with her when her mother read to her. The squirrel in that book had been a bit friendlier, but she supposed that talking animals in books were probably not very much like talking animals in real life.

"Toto, do you think that the squirrel I met was just my imagination?"

"What do you mean, *just* your imagination? Imagining is the best kind of thinking. You should be glad you do it so well."

"You think I do it well?"

"Well, I wouldn't even be here talking to you right now if it weren't for your imagination, would I?"

It was this kind of clear thinking that made Toto her favorite friend. Now that the storm was over, she laid the fox carefully on the pillow next to her head.

"Thanks for being such a good friend, Toto. You always give such good advice."

Toto, who was just dropping off to sleep, murmured one last thought before they both fell fast asleep, "You should see what other interesting creatures might be up in that tree." Those words floated along with Bronwyn as she drifted off to sleep and filled her dreams with…well with strange and wild adventures that she could never quite remember the next day.

In the morning, the sun was shining and the storm was forgotten. As she lay in bed thinking about getting up, Bronwyn suddenly remembered Toto's last thought and jumped quickly out of bed. If there was a talking squirrel in that tree, maybe there would be other interesting characters up there as well. This time she put on shorts.

It was easier to climb up into the tree this time. She swung her leg confidently over the second branch and leaned back against the trunk. It was still the cool of the morning and the birds cheeped and chirruped all over the yard. After a few minutes quiet wait, she began to wonder if the squirrel would come. She didn't have to wait very long. The scratchy sound of a fast, little clawed animal warned her it was coming before the bushy tail came into view, and the squirrel skittered onto her branch.

"Come to look for missing strawberries?"

Bronwyn took a deep breath and closed her eyes while she tried to remember the words she had rehearsed, "I am very sorry that I said you were a thief, and I would like to be friends, please."

It spit a seed out of its mouth onto the lawn below and eyed her suspiciously. "I don't think I have time to just sit here with someone who doesn't seem to do any work. Some of us have to prepare for winter. I have children at home who need their mother."

"Does that mean you're a girl squirrel?" exclaimed Bronwyn with surprise. She wasn't sure why, but she had thought she was a boy squirrel, maybe because her name didn't sound very girlish. (Later, Toto noted that what sounded girlish to a human girl might not be the same as what sounded girlish to a squirrel. You can see why she often consulted the keen witted fox!)

Pert hissed at her and Bronwyn was afraid they were about to have another fight, so she rushed into an apology right away, "I am sorry, Pert, but I've never met a squirrel before, and I don't know how to tell the difference! Also, your name sounds so much like Bert in *Mary Poppins*; I just thought you were a boy. Please don't be mad at me!"

"You don't know very much about your own neighbors."

This brought up the idea that had made her get out of bed so fast that morning. "Are there other animals that live here? Do they talk, too? Can I meet them?"

"Well," the squirrel said thoughtfully, "You might actually be sitting on one right now. I haven't seen the miserable one out and about yet this morning."

Bronwyn squirmed anxiously out of her seat and got on her knees. She looked for any sign of a flattened neighbor all the while wondering how she could have sat on it by accident.

"Who is 'the miserable one'?" Before Pert had time to answer there was a tiny voice at her elbow.

"I suspect she is referring to me." He never sat still for a moment, but marching aimlessly in a small uneven circle she could see a rather large looking black ant.

"Oh, hello. What's your name?"

"Pfft," snorted Pert, "Whoever heard of an ant having a name?"

"It's true. There are so many of us – usually. No time for names."

"Can you imagine how much time it would take to come up with names for every single ant in a colony? They'd never get anything done." The squirrel crept closer and shook its head, "Just think about how hard it would be for the queen to remember the names of thousands and thousands of followers so she could tell them what to do. It's completely impractical."

Bronwyn felt sure this was wrong somehow, and she needed time to think it over. "Well," she said slowly, "In *Winnie-the-Pooh,* even the tiniest of Rabbit's friends and relations seem to have names even if they are just plain ones like 'Small'. We could call you Small."

"Frankly, I'd rather you didn't call me anything at all before you called me that. What did that character do about being called 'Small', anyway? I hope he got some kind of revenge."

"No, but they did find him at the end of that story."

"So he ran away, did he? Can't say I blame him."

"Okay, I won't call you Small, but what should I call you?"

"I'm not sure I know why you're calling me at all."

"I'm new to this tree and trying to make friends."

Pert chimed in to help solve the problem, "You can just call him the ant, he's the only one left in the tree. He keeps looking for his colony, but they seem to have disappeared."

"Really? Your whole family? How did that happen?" Bronwyn felt sadder and sadder for the insect she had nearly sat on a few moments earlier. He had no name *and* no family.

"I don't know," for just a brief moment the ant stopped marching and scratched his head with his front leg, "They just got fewer and fewer and then one morning there was just me."

There didn't seem to be anything else to say to such a sad story, and after a moment the ant marched rapidly away and out of sight up the trunk of the tree.

"He's always depressing to be around. He can't seem to decide what to do without ten thousand others doing the same thing. It's pathetic." Pert was obviously not the most sympathetic person, even if she was a mother. Bronwyn suddenly felt hungry and jumped down out of the tree.

"I'm going in for lunch."

"See, it's easy for you. Your house is always full of food. We never see you running around outside trying to find something to eat," the squirrel was already almost out of sight before Bronwyn turned to wave goodbye. She wandered thoughtfully inside to see about the rest of that leftover lasagna.

IV

Emerald

After lunch, Bronwyn's Mom made her work on her multiplication tables. No matter how many times she tried to think about 6 x 9, her mind kept wandering back to the tree. Finally, in between the 6's and the 7's, she went online and looked up "squirrel".

There were so many different kinds that at first she couldn't decide which one was like Pert. There were some very cute red squirrels with pointy ears, some with shiny black fur and even one kind called an Albino squirrel that was all white. In the end, she decided that it must be a Western Gray Squirrel that she'd met and made friends with, and she read all about them in the article.

"Geroge Ord...what a funny name!" There were a lot of little doorways to other things online, and she was always getting side-tracked. It turns out George Ord was the first man to write about what the Western Gray Squirrel was like back in 1818. Did that mean he was the first person to ever see one? Did it talk to him? she wondered. He had a nice smile, but his shirt was rumpled. She read about how he also described the Grizzly Bear and Pronghorn sheep, but stopped herself from wandering off into any more links in the nick of time and clicked back to the page about squirrels.

She learned that Pert's nest was probably full of babies called 'kits' and that the nest was called a 'drey'. She also learned that the reason Pert's family wasn't living in the big maple tree was that squirrels like her like to live in fir or pine trees instead. The kits would come out of their nest sometime in the spring and summer but would live with their mother for another six months.

"If I lived with my parents for only six months, I would have had to find my own house a long time ago. No more lasagna!"

There was the sound of footsteps from the hall. Bronwyn quickly switched back to multiplication and started seriously trying to remember all the 7's. As soon as the 8's and 9's were done for the day, she could go back outside.

"If there were 7 mother squirrels living in Mrs. Morris' huge pine tree (it was the biggest on the block and stood right outside her window), and they each had 7 baby kits in their dreys, how many squirrels would be living right next door to my house?"

"That's easy, 49." Something made her wonder if she was forgetting an important part of that math problem. She looked out the window at the big old pine and imagined 49 little squirrels poking their little heads out of their nests and sniffing the summer air. Where were their mothers? It was like the book about the baby bird who asked, "Where is my MOTHER?" Wait! There would be 7 sets of 7 babies and that would be 49, but she was forgetting about the 7 mothers! If she added 7 more to 49…she would get…Oh no, wait! It would be 8 sets of 7 if she added in all the mothers! "8 times 7 is…" her brain hurt, "56!!"

When all her work was done, and she'd imagined hundreds and hundreds of baby squirrels all over the neighbors pine tree, she raced upstairs to talk to Toto.

"Come with me, Toto, it'll be fun!"

"Oh, no thank you," the fox declined politely, "I'm so comfortable here on your pillow."

"Why? It's more fun outside."

"No, no, I'm happy here. And dry."

"Is that what you're afraid of? That I'll leave you out in the rain again? I told you I'd never, ever do that again. It was just a one time mistake."

"No, you go and tell me all about it when you come back."

Bronwyn felt bad about bad about leaving Toto in the rain, but really, a few minutes in the dryer and it had all come right again. Almost. Her fur wasn't quite as soft and lovely as it had been when she was new. Maybe she was embarrassed about having matted fur. Maybe... but there wasn't any more time to think about it. The afternoon was slipping away.

Back in the tree it seemed silent and lonely. Pert was nowhere to be seen, and there was also no sign of the ant. The breeze was rustling through the branches, though, and it made a nice sound for thinking to. She looked all around the yard from her perch and then wondered how much else she could see if she was higher up in the third or fourth set of branches. As she climbed she noticed that the branches were getting thinner and bouncier. It made her heart beat fast and she gripped each branch as hard as she could. She wondered what it would feel like to fall all the way down and also what a wheelchair was like.

When she did finally sit down and look around from the higher perch, she saw that the view had now opened out, and she could easily see over the back fence and across the alley and even over the neighbor's fence and across their lawn. She saw cars and electrical poles and people and even the tops of some houses. It was a strange, far-away feeling, and she thought again about being on sailing ship with the whole neighborhood being like the ocean. The moving leaves and branches made noises that almost sounded like whispered words.

Suddenly, there was a scrambling sound, and Pert leapt onto her branch. Bronwyn was so surprised that she jumped and had to grab the branch to steady herself.

"You should give me some warning before you fly in like that," she scolded the squirrel.

"Sorry, but I've never met anyone so clumsy at sitting in trees."

Bronwyn ignored this rude remark and breathed in deeply with her eyes closed. "Do you know, Pert, I feel like the tree is making words with its branches and leaves. It makes me feel strange inside."

Pert looked at her oddly and cocked her head to one side. "What makes you say that?"

"I don't know exactly, I just feel like there are words around me somehow."

Pert had stopped chewing and moving about and was sitting very still. Her eyes glittered as she stared hard at the girl who sat on the branch with her eyes halfway shut. She seemed about to say something, but there was an unexpected flutter and a small branch nearby suddenly bowed and rustled. Bronwyn opened her eyes all the way and looked up. A little bird had just landed and looked quite ready to join the conversation.

"Maybe you need to listen to the words." It was a beautiful bird with a red head and neck. It preened its feathers with its beak.

"Are you a robin?" asked Bronwyn cautiously, hoping he wasn't as easily offended by ignorance as Pert.

Pert chimed in, offended even when it had nothing to do with her, "A robin? For goodness sake, robins have red chests, not heads and necks. And it's quite a different color of red. This is a rosefinch."

It was true that the red feathers were pinkish red and covered the head and neck. The birds, with its head bowed and face all blushing, seemed like a humble and agreeable animal.

"Are you a girl bird?"

"No, he's not a girl bird!" Pert was indignant again, "Don't you know that only the male rosefinch has the red color, the females are only brown."

"Do you have a name? I mean, I know now that ants don't get names, but do birds?"

"My name is Emerald."

"Emerald?" Bronwyn thought carefully back to the week before when she and her sister were looking up different birthstones on the Internet. Her birthday in November meant that hers was the topaz, which was a brownish, golden color. Her sister's birthday in May had meant that the emerald was her stone and she was quite, quite sure it was a dark green color. How odd that a bird with a red head should have a name that means 'green'.

"I know," sighed the finch, "My mother had a sense of humor. It gets better – she named my sister Rosie".

Bronwyn did laugh at that. The red one named 'green' and the brown one named 'red'. She would have liked to have met that mother bird.

"Well, I love your name. Do either of you ever want to ask me my name?"

"We know your name already, we hear your Mom calling you all the time. We hear you outside playing with your friends, too."

"Did you know that my full name means 'guardian of the white-chested bird' in Welsh?"

The others confessed that they didn't and then a silence fell.

"What's Welsh?" Emerald finally ventured.

"It's the name of the language they speak in Wales, which is a country or something."

"Well, is it a country or a something? It can't be both." Pert of course, had to point out the shady little spots in her sentence.

"I can't quite remember. I'll look it up online when I go back inside." She tried not to sound annoyed for fear of starting another argument.

"What's online?"

"Just websites and stuff."

"What's a website?"

"Aaag…don't keep asking me stuff!" She knew she wouldn't be able to answer that one at all.

Pert nibbled on the branch, and the bird kept preening its feathers in the awkward silence. Suddenly Emerald looked up and spoke quite seriously to Bronwyn.

"Before, you were talking about hearing the words from the tree. Can you tell me what he was saying?"

"I don't know what you mean." She looked at the bird and then at Pert who was looking at her sharply again.

"This tree hasn't spoken for many years. We have all tried to hear the words, but he's been silent and sad for so long. None of us were alive the last time he told a story. I think Pert's great-grandmother might have been the last one to hear him speak."

"That's true, as far as we know, she told my grandmother all of his stories up until that very last one and then she died before anyone heard him speak again."

"Maybe he's quiet because he doesn't feel like talking. You don't have to talk *all* the time, you know."

'Yes, but – for years and years? That's either a very long nap or a really long pause. Not even a tree should be quiet for that long," said Pert.

"Huh… a pause…maybe there's a remote control and someone hit the pause button and then forgot to unpause it and it's stuck like that," mused Bronwyn.

The others simply stared blankly at her at this.

"But, why do you think I can hear him speak if you can't?"

"Trees only talk to climbers. Human climbers. Usually they're children. Not all human children who climb trees hear the stories, though."

"Why not?"

"They also have to be listeners."

"Can't any kid be a climber and a listener?"

"I'm not sure. I think my grandmother told me something about it being only certain, special children."

"But the tree told your great-grandmother stories."

37

"No, she just heard them while he told a climber, he didn't tell them to her. It just doesn't work that way."

"Who was the climber?"

"I just remember it was a little boy. He used to come up here and talk to my great-grandmother and also to the tree."

Bronwyn was lost in thought for awhile. Sometimes it seemed like no one listened to her. They were all too busy being grown ups or just bigger kids. She knew what it was like to have something to say and have no one who would take the time to stop and listen. If that was what was going on with this tree, well, then she guessed she could understand why it might be sad and depressed.

Emerald had said little for the last few minutes, and he now hopped lightly to a closer branch and fluffed up his wings.

"You should sit quietly and alone up here and listen to see if you can hear his voice. If you can hear Pert and me talk to you, I think you might also be able to hear him."

The thought of the tree talking somehow made Bronwyn much more nervous than hearing the animals talking. She didn't think she was ready for that. "Okay," she groped around for an excuse to run away, "but right now I'm really tired. I'll come again tomorrow and see if I hear anything." With that, she slithered down the branches and jumped to the ground. She turned and waved to the rosefinch and squirrel. Pert was already scampering away, but Emerald flapped his wings and watched her go back into the house with his head tilted thoughtfully to one side.

V

Liberty and Grace

In the dark, Bronwyn held Toto up to her cheek and waited. She had told her all about Emerald and the mysterious talking tree that no longer talks.

"Well, it seems like this adventure is just getting started," Toto finally said softly.

"Yes, but what if he doesn't talk to me, either?"

"But you said it seemed like you heard some words."

"I know, but I couldn't understand them."

"You should try again tomorrow. Maybe since it's been so long since he had a listener, the tree needs some practice." Toto's voice was unsure; neither of them had any idea what would happen next.

*   *   *

The next morning she crawled back along the largest branch in the third set of branches and sat with her legs down either side with her back resting against the tree's trunk. It was still cool, and none of her other friends were anywhere to be seen.

"Pert?" She waited, but there was no answer.

"Emerald?" She listened for the flutter of wings, but she only heard the rustling leaves in the morning breeze.

"Ant?" She hoped she hadn't sat on him.

Now she started to wonder just what a talking tree would sound like. She had read about some in books. The talking trees of Narnia had voices that matched their kind of tree, like smaller ladies' voices for smaller more delicate trees and big, booming voices for big heavy trees. This tree was a maple and so it would have a big, booming voice. The thought made her nervous. In *The Lord of the Rings*, which Mom was reading out loud to all the kids, the trees talked very slowly and it took them weeks to tell a whole story! That sounded boring.

There was a sleepy feeling all around her like a warm blanket. The quiet murmur of the gently dancing branches made her feel lost, and she floated along on the melody of rustling leaves. Maybe it was alright that she didn't understand the words, in her heart she understood the music just fine.

Beneath the tree, attached to the side of the garage, she saw the bird house where Liberty and Grace used to live. Liberty was the very first pigeon that they had ever had. They had all gone together to the pet store and picked him out. It was an exciting idea that he would fly free all around the neighborhood, but then he would always come home and never fly away from them forever. It was like some sort of strange magic. What would make him come back when he could just fly away and keep flying until he came to a castle in Europe or a beach in California or the top of the Empire State Building? He was more mysterious than any of their other animals and that made him special, even if he was just a common pigeon.

At first, they kept him in his cage and gave him food and water every day. He was still very young and not ready to fly too far. When he was big enough, they opened the cage door and let him out. He walked around on the ground for awhile, but finally he started flapping his wings, and soon he was flying up onto the lawn chairs and up into the tree. Then one day, he flew away.

"He'll come back," Dad promised them, "He's a homing pigeon and this is his home." But he didn't come back. That evening they stood in front of the house and looked out over the valley searching for him, but he was nowhere to been seen. That night, they all sadly wondered whether they would ever see him again.

"Look, is that him?" Mom yelled from the open upstairs window the following evening. She had been the first to see him come home. They all ran outside and called to him, but he sat

43

stubbornly on the neighbor's roof and stared down at them. Then he flew down and walked like a silly bird right down the middle of the street. Dad ran and got the fish net and started trying to catch him. Liberty was now a good flyer, and there wasn't any way he was going back to that cage after he'd had a taste of flying freedom. But, still, he was home, and he did finally have a change of heart and fly back into the back yard to eat his dinner. As it grew dark, he snuggled down into a little fluffy ball of gray feathers and went to sleep in his cage.

After that, Liberty flew off every day. He loved to circle and dive and play in the sky above the house. But everyone agreed; he needed a playmate. They knew pigeons loved to be together in groups, and they weren't meant to live alone. It was back to the pet store, and this time they chose a beautiful white bird with light brown touches on her breast and wings. She was called an Old German Owl pigeon. They took her home and named her Grace.

Liberty and Grace loved each other instantly. Grace was not a homing pigeon, so they kept her in her cage. Liberty came home every night, and they snuggled down together, cooing and grooming each others feather. One day Dad wondered if they were so fond of each other that Grace would stay with Liberty even though she could fly off if she wanted to, so they let her out.

Sure enough, Grace stayed. She mostly spent her days wandering around the backyard. Sometimes she flapped and fluttered her way up to the top of the arbor. Sometimes she would even fly in big circles in the sky along with Liberty, but they always returned together. She had made her home with the family and with Liberty.

One day, Bronwyn noticed that both Liberty and Grace where behaving strangely. They waddled around the back yard and whenever they found a piece of straw or thick, dried grass they would pick it up in their beaks and carry it to their house. After awhile, there was a great pile of tiny twigs and grass. They had made a nest.

It was an exciting day when the kids first noticed that Grace was no longer flying around the back yard so much, instead she sat in her house on her new nest, patiently watching Liberty come and go and eat the bird seed scattered on the patio. Then Liberty would fly in, and they would switch places. Grace went down to eat and drink while Liberty sat on the nest. Everyone waited anxiously for the eggs to hatch.

They waited and waited. One day, they noticed that neither Liberty nor Grace were on the eggs. Why had she left them alone? Why had he given up taking his turn on the nest? Several days later they all had to accept that there would be no babies coming from those eggs. Something had gone wrong. They took them from the nest and buried them under the tree.

Several more times Grace laid eggs, and she and Liberty lovingly cared for them. Each time they eventually abandoned them, and the children took them away. By this time they had gotten four more pigeons. These new birds were all white and they were all very fast, homing pigeons. Soon Liberty was flying with them everywhere they went. Four whites and one grey could be seen every evening out over the valley swooping and diving and racing in ever-widening circles.

Then winter came, and tragedy struck. On a bitterly cold November wind, they saw a huge hawk gliding high above the dead grass and bare trees. One day, a man came to the house carrying one of the whites. He said he had been out on a walk and saw the bird being attacked by the hawk, and he had chased the bird of prey away and rescued the white. Her name was Somono.

After that Somono stayed in her house while she recovered from the wound in her chest. The other birds flew out without her. Sadly, there came a day when only three birds came home. Liberty and two whites. The next day was gray and drizzling.

When Bronwyn looked outside she saw something lying on the brown lawn under the tree.

It was hard to see what it was, but when they went outside they saw that it was Liberty. He was stiff and frozen and quite dead. They looked up into the tree and saw the hawk sitting there gazing down on them. He was a huge bird with long, cruel talons and a sharp, curved beak.

"Why did he do that? Why did you do that?" shrieked the furious children. The bird flapped its wings as if to say, "I don't have to listen to this", and flew away.

They ran back inside the warm kitchen, and Mom said a bunch of things about the cycle of life and natural order and other things that were hard to remember because it's hard to listen to that kind of lesson when you're crying. Later, Dad went out to collect Liberty. Everyone went together into the field across the street and buried him there.

They wondered what had happened to Grace during that horrible afternoon. Even though they dreaded what they might find, they looked around the yard to see if she had been attacked by the hawk as well. There was no sign of her anywhere, and finally they all agreed that she must have flown away. After they went inside to soothe their sadness with hot chocolate, Grace could be seen circling high overhead in the cold sky until at last she flew away to the south in a straight line instead of a circle.

That night, all the remaining whites were locked up in their house, and they stayed there for the rest of the winter. The hawk came every day and sat in the tree looking for the pigeons, but there were no more birds flying free from their yard. Finally, he flew away and didn't come back.

In the cold winter, one of the whites laid an egg. No one thought it would hatch, but it did. No one thought that the tiny little bird would live, but it did. Soon it was obvious that Liberty was the father as its feathers came in all mottled with gray and white. They named him Pursuit.

Bronwyn sighed deeply when she thought about all of these things. She felt like she was waking up from a dream and yawned and stretched her arms. Suddenly, it dawned on her that there were parts of that story that she had never known before. They had always wondered what had happened to Grace. They had worried that she too had fallen prey to the hawk. But in her mind's eye, she had clearly seen her flying away to the south.

Bronwyn held her breath for a moment, and her heart thumped wildly in her chest. She knew in that moment that she had heard the story from the tree who had seen it all take place. It was frightening and wonderful, all at once.

There was a scratching sound, and Pert appeared on the branch. Then a fluttering of wings and there was Emerald. Without any noise, the ant also made his appearance, peeping from under a leaf. They stared at her in wonder.

"Bronwyn, you've woken up the tree."

"I heard him tell me a story! It was a story I mostly knew already, but he told me the parts I didn't know."

"We heard it too. We also didn't know what happened to poor Grace." Emerald shuddered when he thought about that hawk . "Thank goodness she's alright."

"I don't know why we should be sadder about Liberty and Grace, just because they were the human's pets, though. There are plenty of other creatures that get eaten by that hawk all the time," said Pert.

"But Grace was special, wasn't she? I mean, she seemed special to me," Bronwyn replied.

"Yes, she was special. She loved Liberty and she was a good nest builder, but don't you remember how sad she was whenever one of her eggs failed to hatch? She had a mother's heart, and she had to fly away and find a new mate. I hope she's happy, and I hope she has a new nest and eggs that have hatched."

"Pert, that really is one of the nicest things I've ever heard you say."

"Well, I am a mother too, you know. I can understand why Grace was sad and flew away."

VI

The Hall of Rings

"She named you." Toto was filled with awe when she heard about the amazing events of the afternoon.

"What?"

"Remember that book your mother read to us called *The Wind in the Door*? It's just like that; Pert named you. She called you what you really are."

This was a very serious thought and Bronwyn decided to put it aside in some quiet spot in her mind to think about later.

"It's so dangerous outside," Toto buried her face in Bronwyn's neck and shuddered.

"You mean because of Liberty? Yes, but the hawk would never hurt you, you know."

"Why not?"

"Because…" she was about to say "because you're not real", but just before the words came out she realized how mean that would sound, and so she tried to put it another way, "Because you wouldn't taste good to him, I don't think."

"It's because of my ruined fur, isn't it?"

"No, silly dear, it's because you have stuffing inside you instead of meat. Hawks are carnivorous. They eat meat."

"All the same, I prefer to stay inside. What will you do tomorrow?"

"I'm not sure. I'll go back up there, I guess. I'll talk to Pert and Emerald and the ant and see what they say. I hope I hear some more stories from the tree."

The following morning was pouring down rain, and Bronwyn spent the hours catching up on her multiplication facts in between reading about rosefinches and squirrels and black ants on the Internet. By the time she was done she had filled all the trees in the neighborhood with imaginary birds and creatures and bugs in sets of 7's, 8's, and 9's. When the sun came out after lunch, she felt full of facts and questions and was quick to run outside and climb up the damp trunk of the tree. A shower of rain drops that had collected on the leaves fell around her.

"Pert?" she called out. There was a flurry of more rain drops from the branches overhead and Emerald flitted onto the branch.

"She's off burying a nut. We were wondering where you were."

"She's always working and running around."

"Well, she has to find food for the winter for herself and her family," Emerald said.

"Has anyone seen ant?"

"I'm here." There was a tiny tickle on her hand and she nearly brushed the little black creature away without thinking.

"Oh, there you are. Has anyone heard the tree tell more stories?"

"We thought you understood, Bronwyn. Trees don't tell stories to anyone except humans who are both climbers and listeners. You're the only one we know." Emerald didn't sound annoyed and peevish the way Pert did whenever she had to explain things like this.

"So, you can hear him when he talks to me? I don't really understand that, since I can't even remember hearing him myself. I thought there would be some sort of voice, but all I heard were quiet thoughts in my head."

For the first time, the ant spoke up first. He reared up on his back legs and put his front two earnestly on her hand, "You were hearing him from the outside. He is speaking from the inside. If you went inside, you would hear him more clearly."

"Inside? What do you mean?"

"There's a doorway, a kind of gateway that opens for the listeners to come inside. It's a magical place. I know where the entry is. I've peeked inside it, but it's dark and closed. Maybe if

53

you went there it would open. That's what I've heard will happen."

"Is it a door? Do you need a key?"

"I don't think so. Maybe you do need a key, and it's gotten lost, and that's why no one hears the stories any more. I'm not sure."

"Or maybe, there is a magic word instead of a key!"

"Do you know any magic words?"

"Ummm... no."

"I'm not sure the magic door even really exists," suddenly they became aware of Pert who had crept up silently from below. "They always tell us those stories when we're little and still in the nest, but who would still believe them later? No one has ever heard this, or any other, tree say anything. I think it's just a story mother's tell their children. I've told it to my own kits many times."

"What's the harm in going there just to see what happens?" the ant wanted to know.

"How far up is it?" Bronwyn was a little nervous about going up too much farther on the smaller, higher branches, as any sensible girl would be.

"It isn't far. Besides, the doorway would never be somewhere where the listener couldn't go, I don't think." The ant marched upward.

The three others followed. Pert bounded quickly ahead, even though she didn't know exactly where they were going. Emerald fluttered protectively about Bronwyn's head and made encouraging remarks and begged her to be careful. It was, like the ant had said, not that far. As she pulled up the branch where the ant and Pert had stopped, she felt a curious feeling of being much safer than she ought to have felt. The branch they were now standing on was so very much larger than it had looked like from below. It was easy to stand and keep her balance here. The great trunk that towered over her was like an enormous brown wall that reached up higher than she even thought possible. When she looked down, she gasped.

The yard was a tiny blur of green and all of the branches in between were like floating islands. The tips stretched out farther than she could see in every direction. It was breathtaking to see how far the horizon looked from where she stood. Suddenly she remembered one of her favorite books.

"I feel like Alice!" she cried and clapped her hands. She could do that now, because holding on was no longer necessary. She stood at the opening of a great cave in the massive, brown wall with Pert now standing, just as tall as she was, right beside her. When Emerald landed she came up to her shoulder, and the ant came up to her knees like a dog.

"Hey, you guys got big!"

"No, you got small," said Pert.

Emerald fluttered out in front of them and looked them all over. "I think it might be both. She got smaller, we got bigger, but the tree seems like it might have grown bigger, too."

The four explorers stepped cautiously over the rim of the cave opening. All the edges were black and looked like coal, as if the tree had been burned by fire. There were glittering drips of clear, golden liquid suspended from the opening and hanging impossibly down without falling. Inside, the room was large and empty and shaped in a giant circle. The walls were all too dark to see, but the sunlight coming in the doorway lay across the floor. This was the most interesting part of the great hall.

"The floor has stripes on it." Bronwyn put her foot down on the pattern, a little gingerly at first.

"Not stripes! They're rings, the tree's rings," Pert said scornfully.

She wanted to ask about that, but she was afraid of being made fun of again, so she put her hand up to her mouth and said to Emerald, "What does she mean by the tree's rings?"

"That's what the inside of a tree is made of. Every year the tree grows a little bit bigger, and then the winter comes and the tree stops growing so much and sleeps. Every year he grows one ring. The dark parts are where he was going to sleep, and the light parts are where he was growing fast in the spring."

They were very beautiful, and they were wide enough that she could walk along them like a path. All the paths led her in a circle around the shadowy, echoing hall.

"So, this is what you meant by being inside the tree, huh?"

"I heard about this place, but I never really thought it actually existed," murmured Pert. She was a little less cocky than usual. "I can't believe I didn't find it before, it would have made an excellent place to store nuts."

"Don't be silly, Pert," remarked the finch, "You would never have been able to find it without a real listening climber."

"Do you think we'll be able to hear the tree's voice more clearly from in here?"

They all stopped and listened without speaking for a moment and then Bronwyn summoned up her courage and said in a faltering voice, "Hello?" A long silence was followed by a deep yawning sigh and a shifting, echoey creaking.

"I'm here." It was very definitely a voice that rumbled out of the dark ceiling and walls. Not exactly a booming voice, or a

57

soft voice, either. Just very clear and very real. There was no doubt about it; some sort of magic was at work.

"Whoa, did you hear that?" Of course, she knew that they had, but it was scary to even think about answering to the tree itself. Her heart was jumping wildly in her chest, but after a few moments of silence, she tried. "So...hello...tree...My name is Bronwyn."

"I know your name. I've known you ever since you were a baby, and I used to hold up your baby swing."

Wow, the tree knew her name. That was definitely weird.

"So...these are beautiful rings you have here..." She hated not knowing what to say, and everything sounded silly when you were talking to a tree.

"Every ring represents a year of my life. There are over 150 of them because I have been growing here for over 150 years." She couldn't quite explain it later, but the voice was very tree-like and was woven together with creaks, sighs and the rustle of leaves.

Bronwyn walked across the rings toward the wall. "Are the ones on the outside the older ones or the newer ones?

"The farther out you go, the newer the rings are. The ring on the very outside edge, nearest to the wall, is the one from this year. The rings in the center are from when I was just a small sapling."

She walked near to the wall and looked at the path that was the second ring in from the edge. "Is this one from last year, then?" She started walking along it with her hand brushing against the wall as she went.

"That is from last year. In the summer you played under me with your friends, and the boys climbed in my branches. You and your friend Chasey talked about her moving to Tennessee while you played on the swings."

"Chasey was my best friend ever. I can't believe she had to move away."

The ant, who had been marching himself across the ringed floor and then up the sides of the walls and back down again stopped and said quietly, "Chasey's a nice name."

Suddenly Bronwyn had an idea. "Ant, I don't like it that you don't have a name. I'm going to give you one. I'm going to call you Chase."

"Not Chasey?"

"No, silly, Chasey's a girl's name. I think Chase is a perfect name for you, you do seem to always be chasing something."

"Hmmm…" the ant, who was now going to be called Chase, scratched his head with his forepaw like he always did when he was thinking, "I guess I like that name. Yes, you can call me Chase if you want to."

"I still say it's silly to give an ant a name," muttered Pert, "Who would we get him confused with? There aren't any other ants around here."

"Yes, well there aren't any other squirrels around here, either, I've noticed. I wonder why?"

"It's because she's chased them all away," chimed in Emerald, "Squirrels do that, you know. Maybe we should call *her* Chase."

"Why do they do that?"

"There isn't enough food to go around for everyone! This yard is my territory. If I don't chase off the others I won't have enough food for my own children."

"The whole yard?"

"Yes, the whole yard," Pert said shortly.

"So it *was* you that ate the strawberries then!"

The squirrel sighed. "Yes, it was me. I'm sorry, but I do have to eat something. You wouldn't want me to starve to death during the winter, would you? And besides, if you want to keep food safe, you have to hide it, you know. How can you expect to have food for later if you just leave it out in the open like that?"

Now that she thought about it, Bronwyn decided that, no, she didn't want her to starve over the winter. "Well, it's all right, Pert, but you know, you shouldn't have lied about it."

"And speaking of chasing others away, Emerald has done a bit of that himself."

"Emerald, not you! Why?"

Pert was a little bit, a very little bit, kinder when he explained this time. "Rosefinches chase away sparrows and smaller birds from their nests. It's just something that they do."

"Well, if you want to know the truth, humans do it too," Emerald said gently. "I know *you* never have, but the tree will tell you, other humans have done it quite a lot."

"Tree, that's not true, is it?

"Go to the very center of the room and then count out eighteen rings toward the wall," the tree rumbled calmly, "And I'll tell you about it."

She did as he told her and found the path. She put one foot directly in front of the other and began to walk along it.

VII

Kinehut

"When I was a very young sapling," began the tree, "I was small and easily broken. But as the years went by, I grew larger and stronger."

"When I was just starting to be strong and tall enough, a small boy whose family lived nearby started to try to climb up into my branches. He was terrible at it at first, and he fell many times before he finally managed it."

"He should have used a lawn chair...that helped me!" put in Bronwyn.

"He didn't have a lawn chair. There were no lawns then. His family lived in a special kind of house shaped like a tent during the warm months, and during the winter they lived down by the fast parts of the river where there are plenty of fish in long houses that were partly built underground for warmth. They rode horses instead of driving cars. His name was Kinehut, and once he got up into my branches, he quickly became my very first listener. I didn't have very many stories to tell in those days. I was young. He told *me* stories, though, and I learned about his tribe and their ways and their history. His people spent their days hunting and fishing and gathering food to eat. We spent many hours together as he grew up. Soon he was tall enough to swing himself easily up onto the lowest branch and sit as quietly as a mouse in the leaves."

"Do mice climb trees?"

"Well, not very often, come to think of it."

"You should say, 'Quiet as an ant…they don't make very much noise."

"It doesn't have a very nice ring to it when you say that, though," Pert objected.

"When you say something is something or other like something else or other…it's called a metaphor, I think, or is it an analogy?" Bronwyn paused trying to remember, "It doesn't work right if you use a picture that doesn't make sense."

"Do you always interrupt this much when someone is telling you a story?" asked the Tree, "It has been many years since I told stories, you will have to forgive me if I'm a little rusty."

"Sorry, please go on."

"There was a squirrel who had claimed me as her territory who used to scold Kinehut whenever he came to visit, but after awhile she realized it was no use and they became friends. Her name was Kaza. She was not at all as quiet as a mouse. She was a feisty little creature who fought tooth and nail for the right to gather and hide her food in and around this area. If other squirrels wandered into it by mistake, she would hiss and bark at

63

them and chase them away. Kinehut always laughed while he watched these showdowns. Sometimes he would bring along a leather pouch of acorns that he found as he walked along and help her to hide them in various holes and forgotten burrows.

I had just started to feel tall and quite proud. During the spring my leaves had come in fuller than ever before. It was the time of year when my leaves were still green and the nights were still warm when I began to see that all was not well in the world of men.

At night there were groups of the darker men, like Kinehut, who wore fewer clothes and carried fewer guns moving quietly across the hilltop towards the river. I saw that they were Kinehut's family and friends. During the day, some lighter colored men passed by noisily on horseback. I had never seen people like this before. Their skin was very pale, and they spoke very differently from Kinehut's people. They all had the same kind of clothes, and they all carried guns. I was young then, and I didn't understand human wars and soldiers. Actually, even though I've heard many stories about such things since then, this was the only time I ever saw it up close."

"But, wait, they went right through our yard?" asked Bronwyn.

"Remember? It wasn't a yard back then, there were no houses here. I was seeing more and more of the other kind of people every day. The lighter men began to have arguments with the darker men who had been here before them. The lighter colored people wanted to build houses and make farms for food, but the darker people wanted them to go away. Finally, they started to fight.

So, on that day at the end of the summer, just when the sun was going down, I saw Kinehut come racing through the tall grass. I saw that he was afraid, and he was breathing so heavily that he could hardly pull himself up onto the first branch. He climbed as high as he could without breaking my branches and hunched down behind the leaves.

Before long, I saw seven men on horseback come galloping up the hill. Their horses were covered in foam and their guns were out. Their clothes were dirty, and they looked angry. They rode right up under me and stopped. Some of them looked around in the grass, and some looked up into the branches. Kinehut stayed very still and pressed himself against my trunk. I could feel his heart beating. He shut his eyes.

The men looked for a few minutes, but then they started getting off their horses to rest them in the shade. While the horses chewed on the grass, the soldiers talked.

"It was only some kid, we got most of the others down the hill," remarked one of the men as he took off his hat and mopped the sweat off his dusty forehead.

"He might have gone for help. They hide in these hills like rats," another replied.

"Colonel George Wright and six hundred men with guns won't roll over and play dead like that crew in Simcoe. It's time to teach these dogs a lesson they'll never forget." Both the men pulled out leather bags from their belts and threw back their heads to drink. The water dribbled down their beards, and they smeared more dust and grime across their already dirty faces when they wiped it away. They looked almost as brown and tired as the boy they were hunting.

"Unless I'm wrong, this war will be all but over after today. I saw them rounding up prisoners over near the main creek camp, and all the others are either dead or scattered. We should head over there."

"What about that kid?"

"He's probably miles away by now. He's no threat. There isn't anyone left for him to muster, anyhow."

Suddenly, there was a cracking sound and I could feel the branch where Kinehut hid start to splinter and break. I tried so hard to keep him up so the men wouldn't see him. Then something happened that surprised everyone. Kaza, who had been quietly lurking above the men, suddenly made the angriest sounding shriek I had ever heard from any animal and leapt down from her watchful perch. She fell like gray fury onto one of the horse's rump. The horse reared up on his hind legs and neighed loudly. In the confusion, the snapping branch was forgotten and the men cursed the squirrel and tried to kill her with the butt of their guns. She was too fast, of course, and raced away into the grass.

In the end, the men remounted their horses and rode away. Kinehut stayed motionless, crouched on his half-splintered branch for a long time. When night fell and he felt safer, he told me about the battle (later they called it the Battle of Four Lakes) and how his chief, Kamiakin, had ridden out against Colonel Wright and his six hundred men after first defeating a smaller group of soldiers at Fort Simcoe. All the chiefs from the whole valley of Spokane and the hills surrounding it had gone together. The last thing Kinehut saw before he fled up into my branches were the dead and dying lying along the paths and the sight of many of the chiefs being gathered together and marched toward a stream-side camp where the white soldiers had pitched their tents.

Much later, long after Kinehut was forced to move away, I learned about what happened to the twenty-four chiefs that they captured that day. All of them, including Qualchan, Kamiakin's nephew, were killed. Today they call that stream 'Hangman's Creek.' Later, the Colonel called a council at Latah Creek, and they made a treaty about how the dark-skinned people would go and live in a special area that they called a reservation."

"Why did Kinehut have to move away?" Bronwyn asked.

"All of the people with darker skin were forced to move away from their homes and land and live together in a reservation so that they wouldn't bother the white settlers anymore. Kinehut had to go with them. I never saw him again."

"But why couldn't they both live here at the same time?"

"I don't know for sure why humans behave the way they do. I do know that some of them wanted to live together peacefully, but it never seemed to work. They had very different ways, and they didn't understand each other very well. Both sides were so angry that they did terrible things to each other, and that made everything worse."

Bronwyn thought for a moment and then she said, "I have a funny feeling about some of those words you said when you were telling that story. I think I may have heard some of them before. I just can't remember. I think I'll ask my mom."

Pert, who had been chewing on an acorn over by the opening, spoke up, "So, I guess it isn't just squirrels and finches who fight over territory, is it?"

"No," replied the tree, "Life can be hard and people, as well as animals, push against each other while they are trying to survive."

"It's getting late," Bronwyn said as she looked out the gateway opening and saw the sun beginning to go down, "I need to go home for dinner. Thanks for telling us that story, tree. Do you have a name?"

"Trees don't need names." This seemed true. And not sadly true, like she was sad about the ant not having a name. Trees were bigger than names… or something. It was a thought for another daydream on another day.

"You said that Kinehut told you stories. Do you remember them all?"

"Yes, I remember them all."

"Do all the listeners tell *you* stories?"

"All of my listeners have had their own stories to tell, yes."

"Will you listen to my stories someday?"

"I've been waiting for that for a long time."

Bronwyn sighed, "Well, we'll come back tomorrow. Don't forget to leave the door open!"

With that the four friends climbed out of the Hall of Rings (the magic chamber of secret stories had a name, you see, and this also seemed right to her) and found themselves tumbling and slithering down the trunk to the branches below. Everyone had returned to their normal size.

VIII

Timmy and Tommy

When Bronwyn climbed into the tree the next day, she wondered how she would find her way back to the gateway into the Hall of Rings. She needn't have worried, however, because Chase, Emerald and Pert were anxiously waiting on the second branch and together they followed Chase up the same way they had the day before.

Inside the round, cave-like doorway, the breeze whispered across the circling paths and their voices echoed in the still hall.

"Now when I see the rings, I think about all the stories that are hidden inside them," Bronwyn said.

"Which one will you choose this time?" Pert asked.

"Well, how about one from the middle?" she walked to the ring that looked like it was halfway between the center of the room and the wall.

"Good Morning," the voice from out of the air around her didn't startle her this time, and she looked up with an excited smile.

"Good Morning, Tree."

71

"I've been waiting for you."

"I was talking to my Mom this morning before I came out here. I know now why so many of those names you told us about yesterday sounded familiar. They are names of places now. 'Qualchan' is the name of a golf course. 'Latah Creek' is the name of a winery that you can see from the freeway. 'Hangman Creek' is where we went on a nature walk last year. And 'Fort George Wright' is the name of a school that's right across from our favorite bike trail."

"I suppose these days people don't remember who those people were that those places are named after."

"Well, I said to my mom, "Did you know those were the names of people who used to live right here where we live now?' and she was all, like, 'What?' and I told her about those people and what happened to them and she said, 'Wikipedia again?' and I said, no Tree-apedia!"

"It seems like humans are forgetting more and more about the things that happened before their own time," sighed the tree sadly.

"Why do you say that?"

"I used to have more visitors in years gone by. I used to have children who climbed up into my branches and listened to my

72

stories much more often than I do today. I don't see many children even playing outside these days. Not like they used to."

"Why not?"

"I don't know. They just stay inside more now. I don't really know what it is they do inside. Children used to complain that being inside all day during the summer was boring and hot. They loved coming outside and playing in my shade, even when they had real troubles, like when they were crippled and had to use crutches just to get around."

"Can you tell me about those children?"

"Well, now, the ring where you're standing right now would be a good place to start."

Bronwyn looked down on the ring she had chosen in the middle. "What year was this?" she wondered out loud.

"It was 1930. Life was very different then. By that time, your house was here and so was your yard, and, of course, I was here too. The family that lived here had five children. The oldest three were girls, and in 1930 they were almost all grown up. The two youngest were boys, twins, and their names were Tommy and Timmy."

"Tommy and Timmy? Hmmm…" Bronwyn thought a moment and wondered where she had heard those names before. Suddenly she remembered. "Those are the names we found carved into the basement floor when we cleaned out down there! There where also some handprints and a date. I can't remember the date now, but I do remember those two names."

"Yes, Tommy and Timmy loved to help their father with projects, and I'm sure they would have had fun marking their names into the concrete in the new basement floor. They also loved to climb me, and they also played quite a bit around in my shade. They had a bench swing on one of my branches.

They did everything together. They discovered the Hall of Rings together and listened to the stories I would tell them together. They pretended to be Kinehut and Qualchan and played war for hours on hot summer afternoons.

Life was very difficult for people in those days. It seemed like nearly everyone was poor. Their father worked very hard on a road crew, but it never paid very much. The family kept rabbits and egg laying chickens here in the back yard, and they planted vegetables in the front. Every Sunday they had rabbit stew after church."

"They ATE their rabbits?" Bronwyn thought about her pet rabbit, Midnight, sitting quietly in his hutch that Dad had built for him, munching away on the cucumber peels that she'd poked through the holes after lunch, and she shuddered.

"Of course, they were hungry. Their mother sewed all of their clothes, but when there wasn't enough material they patched their old clothes up and kept wearing them, even when they didn't fit anymore. The older girls all still lived at home and helped mother with the house. They helped take care of Tommy and Timmy, but the boys were now nine years old and hated being bossed by so many big people.

It was during this year that something happened that changed everyone's lives forever. It was the early summer, and Tommy started to feel a little stuffy in his nose. He complained to his mother that he felt hot, and she felt his forehead with the back of her hand.

"Go inside and wash your face and hands and lie down for awhile," she suggested.

Tommy's feet dragged all the way up the stairs. He felt so tired. He crawled into bed and slept all through dinner.

The next morning Timmy was taking table scraps outside to feed to the animals when he noticed the door on one of the rabbit hutches hanging open. Sure enough, when he looked inside, there was no sign of the brown lop. He looked around the yard and saw the escaped rabbit sitting quietly under the hedge, munching happily on a cucumber plant. Timmy knew from experience how hard it would be to catch him if he tried to chase

75

after it himself so he called loudly for his brother, who hadn't yet gotten up from bed.

"Tommy!! Come on out here and help!" He knew his brother was feeling sick the day before, but the family couldn't afford to lose a rabbit.

But Tommy didn't come out. Instead they heard him calling out from the boys' upstairs bedroom. Why wasn't he coming? Timmy yelled up at him again and watched as the brown rabbit hopped further under the hedge.

"Thomas! We need your help down here," his mother called out from where she was hanging up the laundry on the line.

Tommy still did not appear, so one of the girls ran up the stairs to drag him out of bed. When they heard her start yelling from the boy's bedroom, everyone stopped what they were doing and stared at each other.

Everyone went running, including the rabbit, which made good his escape by wriggling under the back fence and went racing away down the alley where he was probably caught by one of the neighborhood cats.

At first mother said that when their father came home from work they would call the doctor.

"Mom, I can't breathe...I can't breathe..." Tommy lay on his bed and stared up at them with tears rolling down his face.

He didn't move anything except his eyes, and they were terrified.

Mother ran down the stairs and called the family doctor. When she came back she was moving quickly. She pushed the other children away from the bed and picked up Tommy. She carried him downstairs, and by the time the doctor arrived she had wrapped him in a blanket, and there was no time for talking or explaining as they hurried him out to the doctor's car and sped away.

Meanwhile it seemed like hours before Timmy came out, and his face was white like chalk. He had forgotten all about the rabbit. He climbed up into me and hid his face in his hands while he cried.

"Tommy can't move his arms and legs," He was crying and scared, "they took him to Saint Luke's. They called my dad and he went there from work. No one will tell me what's wrong."

No one wanted to even think about what it could be, let alone talk about it. Nearly every day in the newspaper there were stories about children who had fallen ill with a dreaded sickness that was spoken about in whispers and kept mothers awake at night with worry. Deep down inside they all wondered if Tommy had gotten this terrible disease.

When his parents came home late that night, the family's worst fears were confirmed. Tommy had polio. Around this time thousands and thousands of children were getting sick with polio all over the country. It usually happened in the summer and when it did, the person who was sick was taken quickly away because it was a disease that would spread to others. No one knew what caused the sickness, and no one knew how to cure it.

In the children's hospital, doctors and nurses in white with masks on their faces took care of the many sick children. There were white sheets surrounding the beds to keep the germs from spreading, and some children were placed in special machines to help them breathe.

As the weeks passed the news got worse. The doctors told Tommy's parents that he would probably never walk normally again. He would always need braces on his legs and crutches, if he was lucky enough to walk at all. At night I watched his mother leaning over the kitchen sink with her hands over her face trying not to cry in front of her children.

*   *   *   *   *

Later, Tommy told me about his time in Saint Luke's hospital where he lived for almost a year. It was a very lonely time for him. At first, even his own family wasn't allowed to visit. They would stand on the sidewalk down below his ward and a nurse would roll his bed over to the window. They would all wave and call out to him and he waved back. It was during this time that Timmy decided to be called Timothy.

Many of the stories I heard from Tommy came from his long, lonely days and nights in the hospital for crippled children.

There was an old oak outside the hospital window, but this tree never talked to the children. Tommy heard him muttering to himself in the windy night, and sometimes the grumpy tree scratched with his twiggy fingers on the window pane. It made the little girl in the next bed very scared. Her name was Patty, and she had a little necklace that she used to play with in her hands in the dark night and whisper little prayers while she cried. It was about someone named Mary and something about 'full of grace' and other words that Tommy couldn't understand. He told her not to be afraid, though, and he told her that the tree back home used to tell him stories and that made her feel better. Tommy told her all about Kinehut and Kaza the squirrel. It was good to remember that other children in the world had had troubles before them."

There was also a boy named James in their ward who used to yell a lot. He would always yell at the nurses when they tried to make him walk with braces on his legs. He said he couldn't do it, but then in the nighttime he would crawl out of bed and drag himself around the room and go through the drawers by everyone's bedside table while they slept.

One night, Tommy watched him go over and take the little bead necklace out of Patty's hands while she slept, and he took it back to his bed. That night, he tried for the first time to get up. It was really hard, but he worked and worked and held onto the bed and crawled his way over to the boy's bed after he was sure he was asleep. It took him a long time, but he got that necklace back and put it back in Patty's hands before she woke up. She would have been really sad if it had been missing when she woke up the next morning, so he knew he had to get it back for her."

The tree sighed while he remembered Tommy's stories. "He was like that, you know - a kind boy and always a boy who would work the hardest to help someone else out."

"Later he told me how he and James had had races up and down the hospital hallways when they were both learning to use their crutches. The nurses would laugh and pick them up when they fell. "Almost time, boys," they would promise, "It's almost time for you two to go home!"

"Finally, one day in the spring, Tommy did come home. His left leg was all bent and twisted by the polio, and it was now permanently a bit shorter than his right leg. This made it very hard for him to walk. He struggled to learn how to get up and down the back steps so he could come outside into the sunshine. He still chased the chickens and rabbits around the backyard, but there never would have been any more Sunday stew if it hadn't been for Timothy's rounding them up from the other direction. His family still loved him and they were glad he was home, but it was hard to get used to not being able to move around like he did before.

With everyone calling Timmy 'Timothy', Tommy decided to be 'Tom'. The two boys still did everything they could together, but there were now many things that they could no longer do. For one thing, they didn't ever climb me again or find their way back to the Hall of Rings. Timothy would not go where Tom could not follow.

In the next few years, the two got bigger and stronger. Tom was now using only one crutch because he had gotten so good at getting around with his bad leg. Timothy had gotten a bicycle, and he would ride it to school with Tom balancing on the back, carrying his crutch across his lap.

When the neighborhood children played together, everyone was careful about poor, crippled Tom. At first, they didn't want to play with him. He looked so strange with his body twisting from side to side when he walked. But they got used to him after awhile, and he started joining into their games when he could. When he got knocked down, he worked very hard at not ever crying, and as time went by he got knocked down less and less.

After awhile, the other neighborhood children stopped worrying so much about him and even stopped noticing his crooked walk. He was just Tom who never complained and never wanted to sit on the side while there was a good game going on. At school, though, there were some mean kids who laughed at the way he walked and even though he loved to read, he looked forward to the day when he didn't have to go back.

IX

Timothy and Ethel

When Timothy and Tom were fifteen years old, their father lost his job on the road crew. He had worked so hard for so many years that finally his back was ruined. He couldn't lift the heavy shovels anymore, and he was always hunched over with pain. Now they were poorer than ever, and the boys knew it was time for them to help take care of their family. They dropped out of school, and both of them got jobs at an egg farm just outside of town. It was an hour long bike ride to get there, but they were paid 10 cents an hour and they both got a dozen eggs to bring home once a week.

On their way home from the farm each night, Timothy would stop the bicycle at the green house on the corner of the block and whistle. They had a friend named Ethel who lived there with her parents. She still went to school during the day. She would run outside, and Timothy would give her two of his eggs, when he had some to give. They would talk for a few minutes and then Timothy would ride the rest of the way home, whistling all the way. Tom watched all of this from his perch on the back of the bicycle, and he could tell by Timothy's smile that he was sweet on Ethel.

They worked hard at the egg farm for three years. In the winter, it was almost impossible to ride the bicycle through the snow, and they would have to stop and push through on foot. They left early in the morning before the sun was up and got home late at night when it was dark and cold again. Now they earned more money, though, because in 1935 President Roosevelt had proposed a law that said that all workers had to be paid at least 25 cents an hour, and after several years of arguing about it; Congress passed the law.

Two of their older sisters were married and moved away, and the other sister was still living at home. She worked in a bullet factory that was so busy that they had to hire women and girls because now the country was at war.

On their 18th birthday, Timothy took Tom with him on the back of the bicycle downtown to sign up for the army. Of course, they wouldn't take Tom, with his bad leg, but he still stood in line and filled out the application. It was hard for him to see Timothy all dressed up in his dark green uniform and hat, looking so tall and straight and strong. More than anything, he wanted to go with him to what ever adventure was in store.

Before he left, Timothy spent more time with Ethel. Everyone knew by now that they were sweethearts. She would slip into the back yard in the evening, and they would sit on the swing and talk about the future.

"No matter what happens, we'll always take care of Tom", they promised each other. They dreamed together of buying a house outside of town where they would live and raise a family of their own, but their dreams always included Tom in some way.

"What will he do about getting to work now?" asked Ethel.

"He's strong; I think he could ride the bike himself if he puts his mind to it."

"But Timothy, his leg!" she protested.

"You'd be surprised what Tom can do when he wants to. We've already tried it out. I made a strap that holds his bad leg to the pedal and then the good leg does most of the work. It'll be a bit tricky in the winter, though."

Finally, the day grew near for Timothy to leave. The night before he went, he spent the evening with Ethel on the swing. They made promises to each other and held each other's hands in the moonlight.

"Promise me that you'll be kind to Tom while I'm gone," Timothy said, "He doesn't have many friends. I'll write letters to both of you, and you can swap stories and keep each other company."

Ethel promised.

"Promise me you'll be good to Ethel while I'm away," Timothy said to Tom the next morning as he gripped his hand in farewell, "If there are any spare eggs, stop by and give her a couple for me, would you?"

Tom promised.

As the train pulled slowly away from the platform, the family shouted and waved while they watched Timothy go off to war. "Remember!" He shouted out to his brother, who stood next to the crying Ethel, "Take care of her for me, Tommy!" He kept waving until the train rounded the curve and carried him away to his new life.

X

A Candle in the Window

As they had promised, Tom and Ethel remained good friends while Timothy was away.

For the rest of the summer and all during the fall, Tom rode the bike to the egg farm. It was hard at first to manage with his bad leg, but he got better at it every day. Once a week he stopped at Ethel's and gave her two eggs, one from each of his coat pockets. "It's for Tim's girl," the foreman would say gruffly as he pressed the precious eggs into his hands at the end of the day. They were still wet from being hurriedly washed in the barn trough. "Don't you break them!" he was told.

When letters came from Timothy, Ethel would come over and sit on the swing while Tom sat on the grass, and they compared the stories and messages. She was working all day now at a fire station that had been converted into a bandage rolling center. All day, every day except Sunday, she and 20 other women would sit and cut and roll bandages for the soldiers overseas and package them up to be sent off to the front. The firemen had moved their beds into the fire house next to the trucks to make room for the busy women. In those days, everyone was doing their part for the war.

As winter grew near, Tom found it harder and harder to ride the bike to work. The rode was slippery with ice, and by November there was snow on the ground. Each day he passed by a small grocery store called Patterson's Grocery, and Mr. Patterson would watch him struggle by in the increasingly bitter weather.

One day, it snowed so heavily that Tom had to stop riding and walk the bike through the icy sludge. His head was bowed over in the blowing snow as he trudged by the shop window. Mr. Patterson opened the door of his shop and put his head out into the street.

"Hey! You! Come in here!" he called out. At first Tom didn't understand him, and he stopped and stared blankly.

"Get in here, young man," the grocer urged him. When Tom didn't move he came outside and took the bike from Tom's freezing hands and pulled it inside. Tom followed, confused.

"Well, where do you work? What is your name?"
"My name is Tom, and I'm out at the Darigold egg farm." Tom stood shivering and dripping.

"You can't keep trying to ride this bike all the way out there all winter. You should find a job closer to home. This bike isn't safe…for you …with that," the man pointed at Tom's bad leg.

"Not much work out there, sir. Not that I can do, anyway."

"Well, I want you to work here," Mr. Paterson busied himself wiping down the counters while he talked. It was the end of the day and almost time to close the store. "My son Jim's over in France. I need a boy to stock shelves and sweep up, run errands and mind the store while I'm gone. I've been watching you pass by here every day, and I need someone like you. Someone strong and hard working who won't make excuses. What do you say?" He looked up from his work and gave the boy standing in front of him a quick, keen glance.

Tom could say little, he was so surprised. Truthfully, he knew he couldn't keep up the bike trip to the farm in the snow and ice much longer. The idea of working in the warm, cheerful store seemed like heaven after the long, cold days of shoveling chicken filth and collecting and packing eggs.

Mr. Patterson came from behind the counter again and grasped his hand in a vice-like grip which Tom returned with his own firm handshake. "Leave your bike here tonight," he insisted, "Come back tomorrow morning at 7 o'clock, and we can get started."

"I need to call out to the farm and let them know, sir," Tom could hardly believe how quickly it was all happening. By the time he left the shop, he had a bag full of bread under one arm and an apple to eat on the way home. His touched his cap at Mr. Patterson through the window and happily pulled his collar up to his ears against the cold to walk the rest of the way home.

The weather was too bad now for any evenings with Ethel and their letters from Timothy. He stopped by her back gate, and she would pull on her coat and come to the fence. A few hurried words about any news that either of them had were all they could manage. As the winter grew fierce in Europe, where Timothy was, the letters were less frequent, anyway.

Tom loved his new job at the grocery store. He quickly became well-known to all the customers. At first they called him 'That Crippled Boy', but soon he became known instead as 'Honest Tom' because he was always completely truthful about the things in the store. If a customer wanted to know how old the bread really was, he would tell them the truth. It was the same with the fruit and vegetables. Mr. Patterson trusted him so much he would let him count the money at the end of the day and fill in the store ledger. More than anything else, everyone was always amazed at how strong he was and what a hard worker.

Toward the end of January, Tom began to feel uneasy about how long it had been since he had received a letter from Timothy. One day as he was walking home, he saw Ethel standing out by the back gate, waiting for him.

"Hello, Ethel."

"Tom, have you had any word from Timothy?"

"No, I haven't since just before Christmas," Tom hated to see her looking so gray and worried, "I'm sure it must be the winter that's slowing down the mail. Or maybe the plane carrying the mail was shot down or crashed. I heard about that happening. Or it could be a misplaced mail bag. I'm sure there's a good reason. I've been checking the paper, and I haven't seen his battalion involved in any of the action."

"It's just been so long, Tom, I'm really worried." Ethel's face without a smile didn't even seem like her face at all. She looked tired and worn.

"Are you working too hard, Ethel?" he asked her gently. He knew that the women in the factories and war centers were working long, hard hours before coming home to do all the housework and cleaning and cooking there as well. Ethel's mother was ill and her father was too old to be of much help. He knew that most of the work fell to her.

"No, I'm fine." She brightened her face with an effort and tried to sound cheerful, "How do you like your new job?"

"It's great. Much better than the farm. I wasn't much good on that bike, after all." He laughed. They did the best to make light conversation, and then he walked home. He was looking forward to the weather clearing up so they could sit under the tree again like last summer. He felt sure that by then Timothy would have gotten a letter through the mail, and all would be well.

February passed like a slow, gray dream. There was still no word from Timothy, and Ethel had stopped waiting for him by the gate to ask. He missed seeing her, and he was starting to feel more and more worried about the long silence.

On March 1st, 1942, a serious looking man in a smart uniform came to the door with a telegram. Tom took it wordlessly, and the family gathered silently around him. Even his father forced himself up out of his chair in great pain to see what the message was. But they all had a sinking feeling, and it was the hardest thing in the world for Tom to force his shaking fingers to open that envelope. He didn't want to read the words out loud, so he handed it silently to his sister, Mildred.

It was Tom's sad job to go and tell Ethel the terrible news. He walked slowly down the dark street to her house and stopped for a moment outside the kitchen window. He could see her busily preparing dinner, moving wearily around the kitchen with a wisp of her hair draped across her face. With a deep sigh, he climbed the back steps and tapped on the back door.

Ethel stared when she saw him standing there at the door, with his hat in his hands. He had never come up to the house before; he had never even ventured into the yard. All the color drained out of her face, and she held the door open. Without a word, he followed her into the dining room where her mother and father were sitting. From under his hat he pulled the telegram.

Ethel took a sharp breath and left the room. He heard the door of her room close, and he laid the telegram down in front of her father.

"So, now at least we know," the old man said quietly.

"How did it happen?" asked her mother, who had begun to cry.

"An air transport plane went down in a storm on January 24th. They weren't able to recover and identify the dead till last week."

There wasn't much else to say. Ethel had not reappeared. Tom left as quietly as he had come and went home.

*   *   *   *

For the rest of the winter, Tom did not see Ethel.

After work, he would sit on the swing in the cold and talk with me about Timothy and how much he missed him. He didn't cry too much; he had gotten so used to not crying from his days of being sick.

He said he always looked over to Ethel's house as he passed by in the evening. She would often sit at the kitchen table with a single candle shining through the window that just barely lit up her sad face and the tears she had held back during her long, hardworking day. It made him think about Timothy, and he longed to go inside and sit next to her.

Chapter XI

Cherry Blossoms

It was in the spring, just when the cherry trees were all
blooming, that life began to change again. Tom had spent the
months going diligently to work with his head bent slightly and
the smile missing from his face. The customers and Mr.
Patterson left him alone, mostly, to find his way through the
sadness in his own way. At night, he sat on the swing with his
head down. One warm evening he heard a creaking sound, and
he looked up to see Ethel coming through the gate.

He started up to let her sit on the swing, but she pushed his
shoulder back down and sat next to him on the swing bench.
"It's too damp to sit on the grass tonight, Tom."

In those days young women carried pocket handkerchiefs
with them wherever they went. Ethel's came in handy that night,
but she still needed to borrow Tom's before she got up to leave.
Young men always carried them in their pockets as well.

Tom may not have needed to do too much more crying
about losing his brother, but Ethel still had more tears to shed.
Over the next few months, his was the strong shoulder that she

cried on. It seemed strange and silly to her now that she had ever thought that she or Timothy or anyone else needed to take care of Tom. In the end, he turned out to be the strongest person she knew. She noticed now how much his own family relied on him as well, especially now that his father rarely stirred from his chair in the living room.

Two of Tom's older sisters had gotten married and moved away. He worked tirelessly to care for the house and garden and rabbits and hens. He shoveled snow and coal and carried firewood. He was usually singing while he worked and never complained about how difficult it was to do all of it with his twisted leg. He had discarded the crutch long ago, and had learned to get along without it.

As the summer months went by, the nights were long and warm, and the smiles gradually returned to the two faces that laughed with each other in the moonlight. They watched the stars come out and pushed the swing a little higher and talked a little louder with each passing day.

As the days became cooler, and my leaves began to turn from green to yellow and orange, I noticed a change in the way that Tom would speak into Ethel's ear. As the bright leaves began to flutter noiselessly to the ground, I could see through the branches down to where the two were now sitting side-by-side on the bench swing with their fingers entwined and their heads bent together in quiet conversation.

"Whoa, wait up," Bronwyn broke in, "Is that another way of saying they were holding hands? What? I thought Ethel loved Timothy!"

"She did. Timothy was her childhood sweetheart, and she missed him very much. But he died in the war, and she discovered that she loved Tom too. It happens like that for people sometimes."

"I'm sorry, but that's just weird. How can you love two different people?"

"Well, you can, and life goes on, even after sad things happen. Do you still want to hear about what happened to them?"

"Even if she doesn't, we still do," chimed in Emerald.

"I still want to hear about it, but I don't know if I like it," said Bronwyn with a sigh.

"Well, whether you like it or not, the day came when the last leaf was about to fall from my branches, and Tom gathered up enough courage to tell Ethel how much he loved her.

"Do you mind?" he asked.

"No, of course not, why would I mind?" she laughed.

"Well, would you be my sweetheart even though I have a crooked leg?" he was laughing, but I knew how serious his question really was.

She smiled and put both hands on his jacket front and said, "Much better to have a crooked leg than a crooked heart, Tom dear."

After that came a promise sealed with a kiss.

"Oh my goodness, they're kissing. I can't believe it!"

"I'm just telling you the real story. If you want I can stop."

"No, keep going. What happened next?"

"Well, they got married. It was the Spring again, and they used cherry blossoms from the tree in her backyard for flowers. She made her own dress, and when they got home from the church after the wedding, they moved into the rooms upstairs here with Tom's parents and older sister, Mildred."

"Yikes, why didn't they get their own house?" Bronwyn had always thought you got your own house after you got married.

"Remember how they were so poor before the war? Well, they were still pretty poor afterward, too. It was like that for many people back then. They liked living here, though, because it was close to Tom's job, and they could take care of his parents. His dad was getting older and sicker, and his mother needed help.

98

They lived there all during the final years of the war. After her marriage, Ethel's parents went to live with her older sister in Idaho. In August, Tom's father died of pneumonia. Mildred stayed home to care for the house while Tom continued to work at the grocery store, and Ethel went every day to the fire station.

By the time the war was over in 1944, Tom and Ethel were ready to go and live in a place of their own. Mildred would stay with mother. On the day that they left, Tom sat in the old swing with his daughter Betty nestled in his lap.

"It's so weird hearing about Tom being a Dad," Bronwyn shook her head. "Didn't that seem just...weird?"

"It's not so strange when you've lived as long as I have."

"Was she a cute baby?"

"She was, and she clutched his shirt collar and stared up into the green leaves with big smiling eyes that reminded me of Timmy and Tommy when they used to lay in a swinging cradle under my shade. She had her mother's smile, though, and she loved hearing her daddy sing and tell stories.

He told her all about the times he had spent with Timothy up in my branches and about the Hall of Rings and the stories about Kinehut and the others. She was too little to understand, of course, but I think it was his way of saying good-bye to me and to tell me that he would never forget the times we had together.

He sang a little song to her that she always loved to hear at bedtime. Tom used to make up songs while he worked, and he had made this one just for his little girl. It went something like this [Bronwyn was sure that she had heard the tune before. It sounded very much like "Oh My Darling Clementine"]:

In the sunshine,

In the moonlight,

In the morning

Of your smile,

I will hold you

Here forever

Gently rock you

All the while.

Don't you cry now,

Don't feel sad now,

Find a place to

Sigh and sleep.

Listen to my

Singing story,

Listen to my

Sorrows deep.

In the cold night,
In the darkness,
I had dreams of
Your dear face.
Smiling angels
Whispered always
Tender mercies'
Promised place.

Like the silver
Bells from heaven,
Like the silver
Singing stars,
You're the candle
In the window,
You're the way home
From afar.

There was a silence as the last words faded away into the whisper of rustling leaves.

"Didn't you ever see him again?" Bronwyn had been wiping away tears for the last several minutes and hated to have the story end so suddenly.

"I saw them again. Not often. Once, when Tom and Ethel had four children, they brought them by to see their Auntie Millie and Grandma. Mildred had baked a chocolate cake and they all ate it on a picnic blanket in the shade. The children's faces were stained with tears, but the cake soon cheered everyone up."

"Tears? Why were they crying?"

"That afternoon they had taken the children to get the new polio shot. In the years since Tom had been sick as a child, people had been trying and trying to find a way to keep more children from getting sick. Up until this point, no one had succeeded and every year thousands of more children became ill, were crippled, and some even died. It was an exciting day for Tom and Ethel when they read in the newspaper that a special plane was scheduled to fly from Detroit to Spokane with a load of vaccinations just for the children of this city. Ethel had always worried that someday one of her children might get sick and suffer like her Tom had, so many years before."

"I wonder if I had that shot? I had a whole bunch of shots when I was little."

"You probably did. I haven't seen any children crippled with Polio in many years."

"So, was that the last time you saw them?"

"I saw them once more when Tom's mother died, and they packed up Aunt Millie to come and live with them in their new house in the country. Tom was bald on top, and his children had grown so tall and strong. The boys climbed the tree, and Tom said good-bye one last time before they left."

Bronwyn sighed with contentment. "I thought that I would bring my books up here to read my favorite stories; I never knew there were so many stories already here!"

Everyone was quiet while they climbed down out of the tree that afternoon. Bronwyn went inside and snuggled down with Toto for a nap.

"Toto, did you know that Tom thought that the stars were like candles in the window of heaven to remind us of the way home? I'll have to try and remember all the words to his song so I can sing it for you." She yawned. "I would love to hear those silver bells from heaven."

"I have so many things to tell you about, Toto dear, but right now I am SO tired." She drifted to sleep and dreamed about a man holding a tiny baby girl and rocking her gently on a swing that hung from the bough of a huge maple tree. She thought she could hear the words of the song floating across to her from out of the past... *Like the silver*

Bells from heaven,

Like the silver
Singing stars,
You're the candle
In the window,
You're the way home
From afar…

XII

The Silver Bell

This time, in spite of the fox's fears, Bronwyn took Toto with her up into the tree.

"Don't worry, I won't forget you outside again," she promised, "I really just want you to meet all of my new friends."

Toto was too nervous to say much when she was introduced to the others. They were polite but much more interested in going back up to the Hall of Rings.

Inside the cool, shadowy room, Bronwyn paced slowly across the curving pathways.

"Good Morning, Bronwyn," the tree stirred to life and stretched and creaked in his old bones.

"Good Morning, Tree," she replied, "I brought Toto to see you."

"Good Morning, Toto, it's nice to meet you. I remember seeing you once before, on a rainy night when you were left outside by accident."

"Well, that's bringing up a sore subject," said Bronwyn.

"They put me in the dryer after that, and my fur was ruined."

"Well, never mind. Even with matted fur, you'll last longer than any real fox out in nature will."

"Really?" said both the fox and her owner together.

"Really. A live fox will only live about 3 or 4 years in the wild, but a creature like you will last almost forever. You'll probably still be around when Bronwyn has children of her own, if she's careful with you."

"I will be, I promise."

"No more nights out in the rain?"

"No more of that, I said I promise!"

Bronwyn felt that a change of subject would take Toto's mind off her past troubles with the wild outside. "We were wondering about hearing another story today."

"Are all of your stories just about human children?" Pert wanted to know.

"No, I actually have a story about a creature that would interest you, Pert, if you stand in the very center, in the first of my rings."

Emerald, Pert and Chase stood crowded around Bronwyn while she stood on tip-toe in the very center of the room with her feet covering the middle dot that was the tree's first ring.

"Long ago, there was a huge maple tree that stood over where the green house on the corner is now. It was very old, and

106

many generations of squirrels had spent busy summers in its branches. Every year, there were fights over who would control that territory. There was a family of squirrels that had always been successful in driving away challengers and keeping the bountiful harvest to themselves and their children. In the year that my story starts, the chief mother squirrel who ruled the big maple was named Zip. She was a fierce fighter and a great mother to many healthy squirrel children.

Every spring, Zip would start to hunt for acorns and berries and seeds and begin to stash and hide her store of food for the coming winter. Some of it she tucked inside the holes that the woodpeckers had made and abandoned. Some she buried in the ground all around her territory."

"Why didn't she just hide it one place, so it would be easier to find later?" Bronwyn wondered.

"Because if you hide it all in one place and someone else finds it, they'll take it all and you'll have nothing to eat during the winter, and your babies will die," Pert explained.

"Zip was always careful to hide much more food than she or her babies would ever need because she knew that sometimes other animals would find her hiding places. Sometimes, the snow would bury the spots where she'd put it, and it wouldn't melt completely until it was too late."

"What do you mean by too late?"

"Once an acorn or a seed sprouts and starts turning into a plant instead of just a nut, a squirrel can't eat it. Zip always made sure that she could get to enough food no matter what happened.

Well, this particular year, she had already started hunting and hiding for another winter when one of the seeds she had hidden the year before sprouted and poked its head out from under the melting snow and dead grass. Like so many of the other trees on this hilltop, I was once a forgotten seed from Zip's hoard."

"Wow, Pert, it was a squirrel just like you that planted this tree! Maybe it was your great-grandmother."

"It was Pert's great-great- and far too many greats to count or remember – grandmother. She was also the great-great- too many greats to remember- grand-daughter of the squirrel who had stashed and hidden the seed that became my mother tree."

"So that tree where your seed came from was your mother tree? What happened to her?"

"Many of the trees in this area were felled by humans to build their houses with. But they left my mother tree standing and built their houses in her shade. She was such a magnificent giant. One year, when I was still quite young, she was blown down by a severe storm. The man who lived in the house nearby cut up the wood and made furniture from it. He made many beautiful pieces for his family. The beds and tables and even toys that the children played with stayed in that house for many years. After the old man died, his children had a sale, and many of the things were sold to neighbors and strangers. One old front porch bench swing was sold to the family who had just moved in down the street, and they hung it from chains in their backyard from the strong arm of an old tree there."

"Oh my! Was that the bench swing that Tommy and Timmy played on and Ethel sat on when they fell in love?"

"It was the very same."

"What ever happened to that swing?"

"Wood from a tree that is dead never lasts forever, especially in the rain and snow. It finally rotted and fell to pieces and was burned in the fireplace."

"How sad. Were you really sad to see that happen?"

"No, it isn't sad; it is just a part of the life of a tree. Lots of new trees come from one old mother. No tree lives forever."

"Have you got any tree children that have grown up because Pert forgot to find the seeds and eat them?"

"Many of the seeds that Pert and her mother and grandmothers have forgotten have turned into little trees, but the humans never let them grow up these days. They pull them up like weeds and cut them down with those loud machines you use to cut the grass. There just isn't room enough for all the people and the roads and cars as well as all kinds of huge leafy trees, I suppose."

"I wish there were more trees," sighed Bronwyn.

"Humans don't seem to need trees as much anymore. They don't seem to care if their houses are in the shade; they have those machines that keep them cool in the summer, and they don't burn wood to stay warm in the winter. The children almost never come outside to play, so they don't need to have the trees to climb or the shade to be in. They think that our falling leaves are a nuisance in the autumn, and they are annoyed by the squirrels who come to collect the seeds. I suppose it won't be long before they cut us all down."

"But I learned in science that the trees drink the poison out of the air. What would happen if there weren't any more trees?"

"Do they still teach children that? Well, I am glad to hear it. I was beginning to wonder if humans even remembered what makes the air good for them to breathe."

"I won't ever forget anything about trees, now," Bronwyn said firmly, "I will remember the trees and also all the people who've lived around them and played in them and hid in them and made things from them and sat in their shade and climbed in their branches and listened to them tell stories. Okay, wait a minute, here's a little story. My mom told me that when she was a girl she used to climb up in a tree in her *front* yard. It was called a Jacaranda tree, and it made the most beautiful seeds that were black and shiny and shaped like big, fat coins. It had purple flowers in the rainy season and had the best climbing limbs ever – they were shaped just like seats! The tree branches went out over the dirt road, and she would hide up there and watch people go by underneath. See, she was kind of like me!"

"That's a nice story, but it's really your Mom's, not yours," the squirrel pointed out.

"Hmmm… I guess you're right. Okay, here's one, once we were camping outside in the yard, and I woke up in the middle of the night, and I heard a creepy noise outside the tent. I'm not sure what it was, but it was definitely creepy."

"Probably just Ranga and his gang."

"Who's Ranga?"

"There's a whole pack of raccoons that live across the street in that empty field. Ranga is the biggest, and he's their leader. You don't mess with him! They always come over here at night looking for food out of your garbage can… or plums from the plum tree. They love those."

"And they drink out of your fountain. Raccoons love water," added Emerald.

"Do you think they're the ones who popped our blow-up swimming pool? We set one up out here, and the next morning it was all flat and the water was gone. I was so mad!"

All three of the creatures and the tree burst out into the strangest kinds of laughter. "Oh yes, we remember when that happened" said Chase, "You've never seen such surprised and disappointed raccoons!"

"Honestly, I don't think I've ever seen raccoons, period."

"You need to sit in the dark sometime and wait quietly. You'll see them all right."

"It's a good start to a great story, Bronwyn," the tree said kindly, "I hope you think of some more for me."

"I could make up a song about it. It could go, like...

In the cold night
In the darkness
I had dreams of your creepy face
It was hairy, it was scary,
Then I nearly lost the race...

The others nodded politely, and there was a little silence.

"Yeah, I can see that I need to work some more on that."

"I really thought it was that mean old hawk who popped my pool."

"The hawk's name is Atra, by the way."

"What? That awful thing had a name?"

"Of course, he still does. He comes from a fine old family that has lived here for many generations. He is the son of Para, who I knew quite well."

"How could you be friends with that horrible bird? Don't you know he killed Liberty and Somono?"

"Yes, I know that. It is his way. It is the way of all hawks and birds of prey. Do you think I dislike Emerald because she feeds on worms? I know all those families, too, you know. They make their cities down in my roots and we really are quite close."

"Blech. Worms. I didn't know anyone could be friends with worms. Oh gross! That means that you have worms living down in your toes! YUCK!"

"You can be friends with anybody if you put your mind to it. I have learned that in all the years I've been standing here."

She reached into her pocket and pulled out a little silver bell that she'd brought from inside the house. "Look here, I brought a silver bell, and I'm going to tie it to one of your branches, just like those girls did in *The Wind on the Moon*. That song that Tom made for Betty made me think of it."

"Is that one of your book stories?"

"Yes, these two girls tied bells to the branches of an apple tree the night before their father went away, and it made a concert of music in the windy night. I want to see if it will work the same with you." She left the Hall of Rings and scrambled out onto the branch. She climbed up higher than she'd ever gone before with the silver bell clutched in her hand.

Bronwyn leaned out on the narrowest branch she thought could hold her weight and pulled out the piece of ribbon she had stowed in her pocket. She fought to keep her balance while she tied the bell to the end of the twig. She was just remembering the story about Kinehut when she heard a sickening crack. Suddenly, she slipped from the broken limb, and as she tumbled off of the narrow branch, she heard the wild jangling of the silver bell.

*   *   *   *

"Bronwyn! Bronwyn! Wake up!!" she heard familiar voices jostling around her head like a dream.

"Bronwyn, what are you doing laying here?" she could see the fuzzy faces hovering over her like clouds.

"Did you fall out of the tree?" she realized now that it was her oldest brother who was staring down at her.

"We just got home and we saw you laying out here; it looked like you were asleep," her sister said.

"Look, you've got Toto under your head. Were you using her as a pillow?"

Bronwyn slowly sat up and looked around her. Sure enough, Toto was laying there in the grass where her head had been. She looked down at her legs and saw scratches and cuts and she wondered, how she did get down there at the bottom of the tree? Where were Pert and Emerald and Chase?

"Bronwyn, are you alright?"

She nodded but said nothing. Was everything a dream? Did she ever really climb the tree and hear the stories? It all seemed misty and far away.

Suddenly, from high overhead, she heard the sound of a tinkling bell. She looked up and saw a flash of silver that glimmered among the green leaves, and she breathed a sigh of relief. She could hear the sound of the music, and in her heart she understood the words. All the secret stories and the memory of her friends flooded back to her from the corners of her mind where they had been safely hidden, and she knew that her adventure had been real. She opened her mouth to tell her

115

brothers and sister about it all, but something made her change her mind, and she closed it with a smile. She would keep the stories and songs hidden for awhile in a secret place inside - in her own Hall of Rings buried in her heart.

"And all the rings, even though there aren't very many of them yet, will hold all of my stories, and all of the stories I heard from the tree, and all the stories I read in books, and they'll all live together in a place that grows magically huge whenever someone crawls inside."

The big kids had already gotten bored with the whole thing and were tramping back inside for lunch.

"C'mon Bron, and don't leave Toto out again," they reminded her.

But Bronwyn sat in the warm grass and tried to remember that little song she'd been trying to make up with her story. It was hard, and there were little bits and pieces of it scattered around in her head.

"I need a little bead necklace to help me remember, like Patty had," she said to herself.

"Oh, ho ho…Brownyn," taunted her brother, "You missed out on SO MUCH fun at camp! It was totally awesome!"

"Yeah, well, you missed out on some fun here too, you know," she replied.

"Oh *really*, like what on earth happens around here that's any fun?" he laughed back.

"Well, quite a lot, really. A lot has happened around here that you don't even know about, so there!"

"You are so full of it," he said, shaking his head, "You're just so making that up..."

"No, I'm not, but for your information I'm not going to even tell you about it."

"I don't even want to hear about your stupid stories anyway, they're just dumb!"

Bronwyn almost said something mean back, but then she thought about Timmy and Tommy and how awful it would be if one of your brothers or sisters went away for a whole year, or even forever, instead of just a week, and she stopped herself. Anyway, she wanted to keep all the stories secret for now. She and Toto could always tell them to each other. And of course, there were always plenty more rings that they hadn't yet even begun to explore. She just smiled a secret smile and had the last word before she went upstairs to her room, "Too bad for you, I ate the last piece of lasagna for breakfast!"

And there was really nothing at all he could say to that!

About the Author

Heather Edwards lives in Spokane, Washington with her husband, four children, and a menagerie of animals. She graduated from California State University at Long Beach with a bachelor's degree in English Literature and from Eastern Washington State University with a master's degree in Education. She teaches part-time at Spokane Community College and homeschools her kids.

You can contact her at **hetoame@gmail.com** or on Facebook at *Bronwyn Climbed the Tree.*

Made in the USA
Charleston, SC
05 July 2011